For Isa,
who asked for a story

The Short Giraffe

Neil Flory & Mark Cleary

No swamp
mail please

Albert Whitman & Company
Chicago, Illinois

Boba the baboon had come to take a photo
of the tallest animals in the world.

The giraffes were very excited.
They wanted it to be perfect.

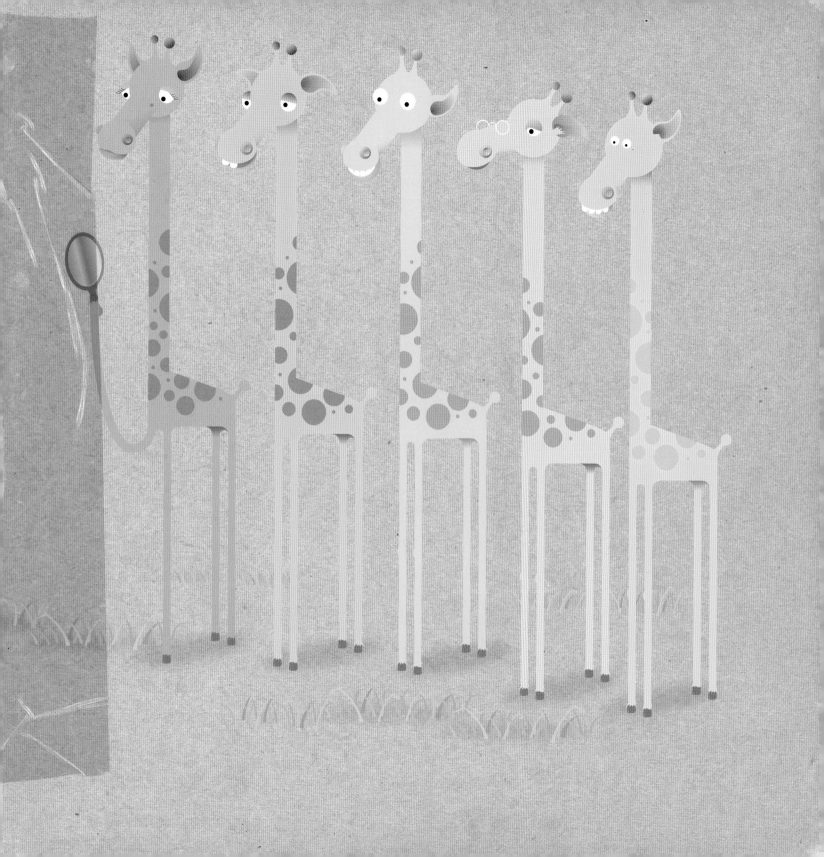

And perfect it was...

except for one
tiny problem.

"Who's that?"

It was Geri, the shortest giraffe who ever lived.

"I'd better stay out of the photo," said an embarrassed Geri.

"I don't want to ruin it for the rest of you."

You still look tall to me.

"Out of the photo?
Don't be silly," said Stretch,
the tallest of the giraffes.

"We'll just have to find a way
to get you up to our level."

So they tied Geri to stilts, but...

he bobbled...

he wobbled...

and

cRASHED

to the ground.

They stacked him on turtles,

but the

shells were

too

round.

They hung him from branches,

but he was upside down.

They filled him with helium, but he floated away.

They tried giving him wings,

but giraffes aren't made to fly.

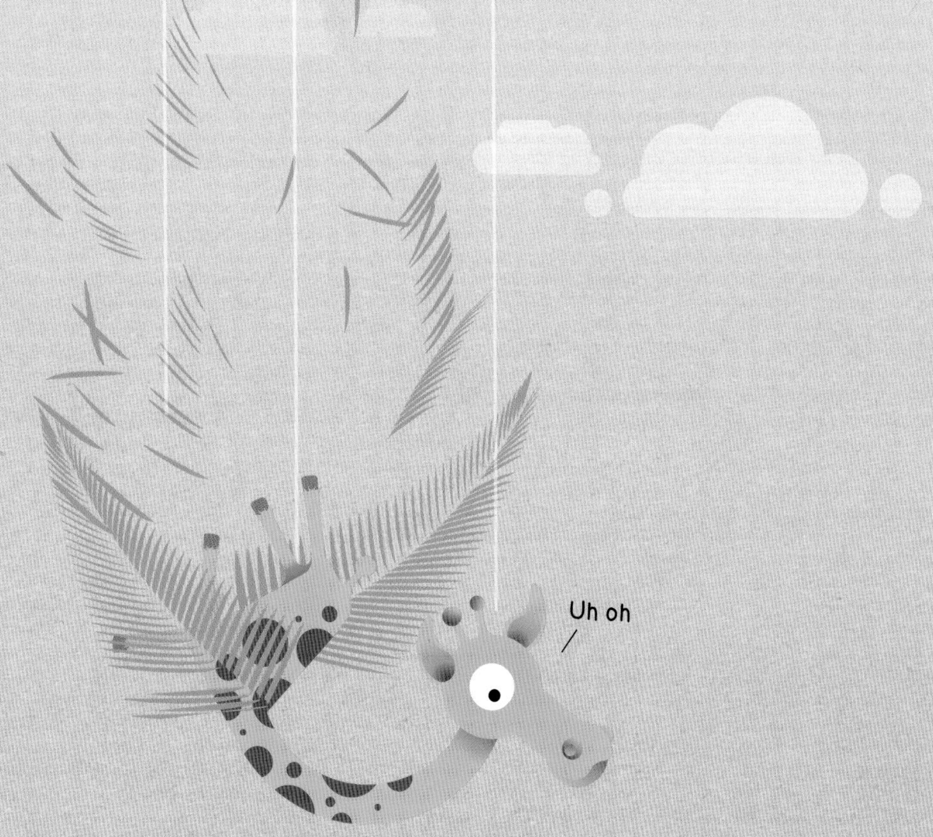

They even tried springs,

but Geri just bounced...

and bounced...

and bounced all around.

The giraffes had run out of ideas.

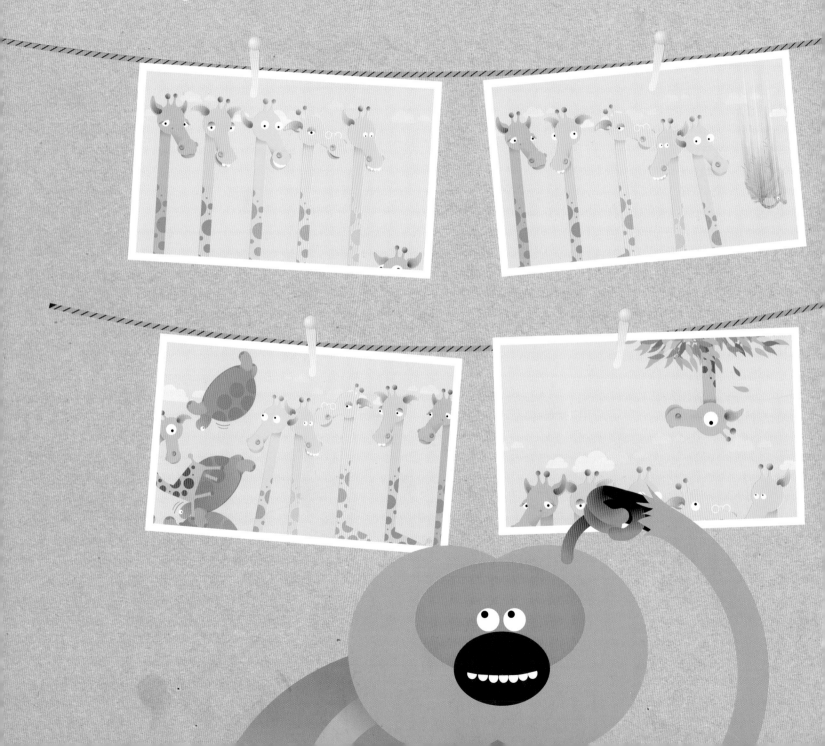

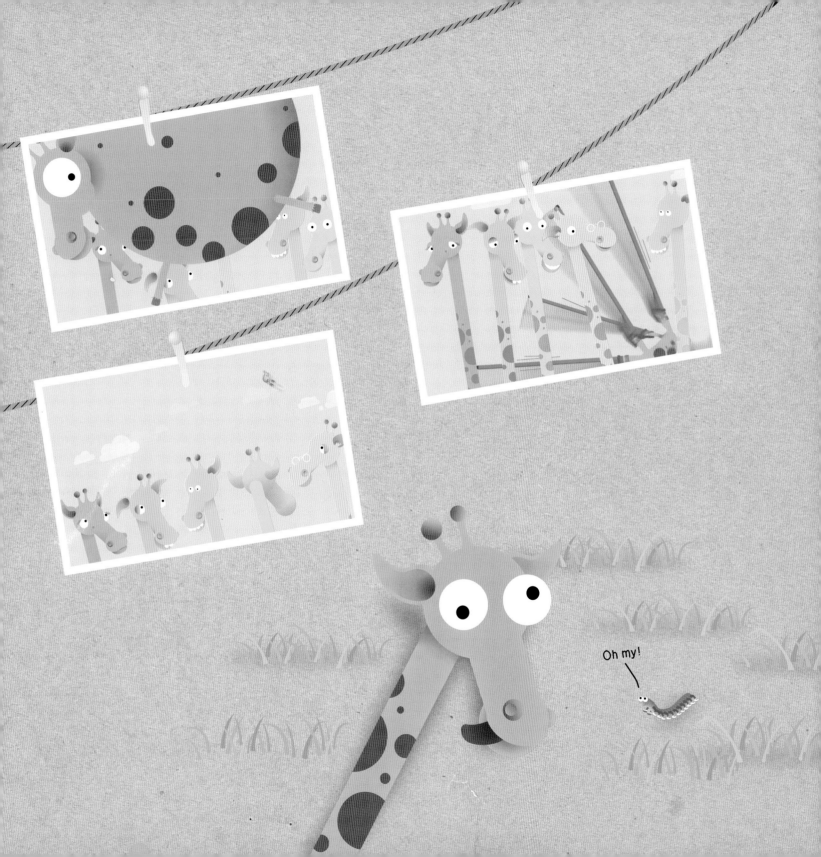

Then a caterpillar who'd been watching
the whole thing finally spoke up.

"Excuse me, giraffes, if I might say,
instead of trying to get
Geri UP to your height...

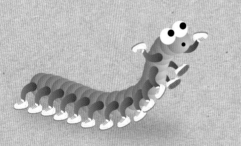

wouldn't it be easier
if you bent DOWN to his?"

The giraffes knew at once that the Caterpillar was right.
They got ready for the photo one more time.

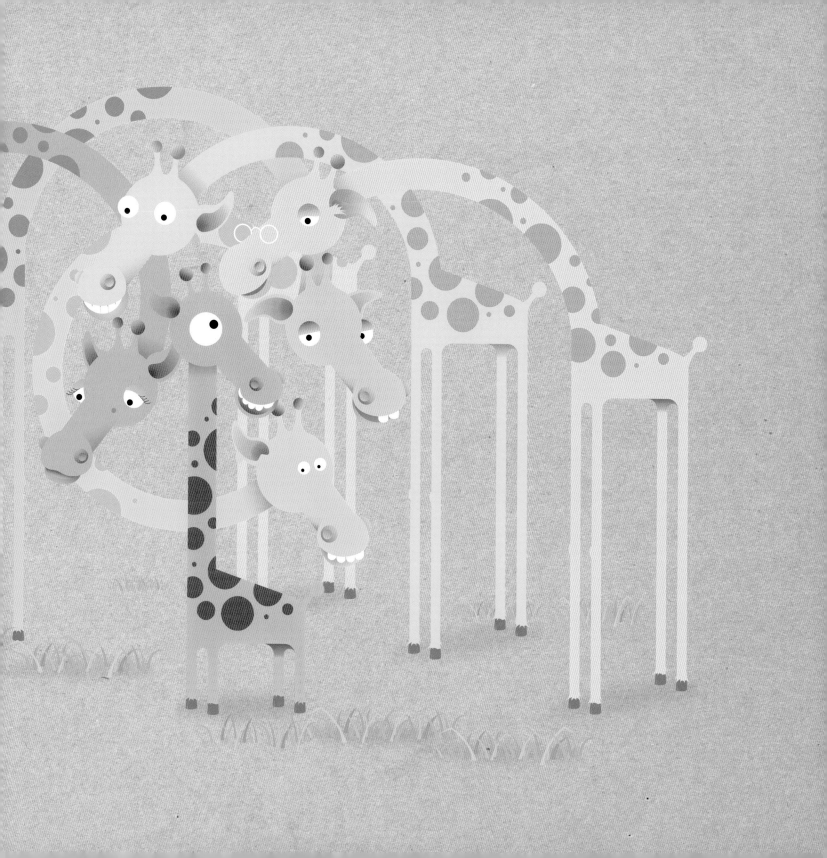

And it was the most
perfect photo ever.

Library of Congress Cataloging-in-Publication Data
is on file with the publisher.

Text copyright © 2013 by Neil Flory
Illustrations copyright © 2013 by Mark Cleary
First published in Australia by Allen & Unwin

Published in 2014 by Albert Whitman & Company

ISBN 978-0-8075-7346-4

Printed in China.
10 9 8 7 6 5 4 3 2 1 BP 18 17 16 15 14 13

Cover and internal design by Mark Cleary

For more information about Albert Whitman & Company,
visit our web site at www.albertwhitman.com.